Tadpoles

Thank you for using your library

DALGETY BAY
07/19

−5 SEP 2019
⟶ DB

1 6 MAR 2018   APR 2019

Renewals can be made
by internet   www.onfife.com/fife-libraries
in person   at any library in Fife
by phone   03451 55 00 66

ON
AT FIFE
LIBRARIES

Thank you for using your library

First published in 2007 by
Franklin Watts
338 Euston Road
London
NW1 3BH

Franklin Watts Australia
Level 17/207 Kent Street
Sydney
NSW 2000

A CIP catalogue record for this book is available
from the British Library.

ISBN 978 0 7496 7157 0 (hbk)
ISBN 978 0 7496 7300 0 (pbk)

Series Editor: Jackie Hamley
Editor: Melanie Palmer
Series Advisor: Dr Hilary Minns
Series Designer: Peter Scoulding

Printed in China

Franklin Watts is a division of
Hachette Children's Books.

For Auntie Sue – S.M.B.

My Auntie Susan

by Sheila May Bird

Illustrated by Daniel Postgate

W
FRANKLIN WATTS
LONDON•SYDNEY

Sheila May Bird

"I like writing,
reading too,
and eating cake
with Auntie Sue."

Daniel Postgate

"I have a few unusual
relatives, like my
brother, Kevan.
He lives in a hut
in India and spends
his time writing
poetry."

My Auntie Susan – what is she like?

She wears a top hat
and she rides on a bike.

She has lines on her face, but I don't think she's old.

She wears a long scarf,
even when it's not cold.

She likes to cook,
she likes to bake.

Her favourite food is
upside-down cake.

Sometimes she gets
in a bit of a muddle.

13

Her favourite food is
upside-down cake.

That's when she needs
a bit of a cuddle.

19

I like my Auntie, as
I'm sure you can see ...

21

Because Auntie Susan
is a lot like me!

Notes for adults

TADPOLES are structured to provide support for newly independent readers. The stories may also be used by adults for sharing with young children.

Starting to read alone can be daunting. **TADPOLES** help by providing visual support and repeating words and phrases. These books will both develop confidence and encourage reading and rereading for pleasure.

If you are reading this book with a child, here are a few suggestions:

1. Make reading fun! Choose a time to read when you and the child are relaxed and have time to share the story.

2. Talk about the story before you start reading. Look at the cover and the blurb. What might the story be about? Why might the child like it?

3. Encourage the child to reread the story, and to retell the story in their own words, using the illustrations to remind them what has happened.

4. Discuss the story and see if the child can relate it to their own experience, or perhaps compare it to another story they know.

5. Give praise! Remember that small mistakes need not always be corrected.

If you enjoyed this book, why not try another TADPOLES story?

Sammy's Secret
978 0 7496 6890 7

Stroppy Poppy
978 0 7496 6893 8

I'm Taller Than You!
978 0 7496 6894 5

Leo's New Pet
978 0 7496 6891 4

Mop Top
978 0 7946 6895 2

Charlie and the Castle
978 0 7496 6896 9

Over the Moon!
978 0 7496 6897 6

My Sister is a Witch!
978 0 7496 6898 3

Five Teddy Bears
978 0 7496 7292 8

Little Troll
978 0 7496 7293 5

The Sad Princess
978 0 7496 7294 2

Runny Honey
978 0 7496 7295 9

Dog Knows Best
978 0 7496 7297 3

Sam's Sunflower
978 0 7496 7298 0